THIS WALKER BOOK BELONGS TO:

_____

_____

_____

FOR SIMON

First published 2006 by Walker Books Ltd
87 Vauxhall Walk, London SE11 5HJ

This edition published 2007

10 9 8 7 6 5 4 3 2

© 2006 Charlotte Voake

The right of Charlotte Voake
to be identified as author/illustrator
of this work has been asserted
by her in accordance with the
Copyright, Designs and Patents Act 1988

This book has been typeset in Godlike

Printed in China

British Library Cataloguing
in Publication Data: a catalogue
record for this book is available
from the British Library

ISBN 978-1-4063-0523-4

www.walkerbooks.co.uk

WALKER BOOKS
AND SUBSIDIARIES

LONDON · BOSTON · SYDNEY · AUCKLAND

Hello

Twins

CHARLOTTE VOAKE

Here are the twins.

This
is
Charlotte.

This
is
Simon.

They're not like each other at all.

Simon loves
his food.
He eats
every single
thing on
his plate.

Charlotte
prefers to suck
her thumb
and stare out
of the
window.

Charlotte
likes
building
things.

Simon
likes making
them fall
down.

Here they are on the seesaw –
one on the ground ...

and one in the air!

Simon and Charlotte
love drawing.
Simon draws
the same patterns
over and over
again.

Charlotte copies
the numbers on the clock.

Simon and Charlotte love books.
Simon looks at the pictures.

Charlotte puts in
some pictures of her own.

Sometimes they take their toys
for a walk in the pram –

Charlotte like this ...

and Simon
like this!

Simon and
Charlotte

don't look
much alike.

Charlotte
and Simon
do everything
differently.

But upside down
or the right way up ...

in the air
or on the ground,

they're happy.

They're
the twins ...

and they like
each other
just the way
they are.

Hello Charlotte.
Hello Simon.

HELLO
TWINS!

WALKER BOOKS is the world's leading
independent publisher of children's books.
Working with the best authors and illustrators
we create books for all ages, from babies
to teenagers – books your child will
grow up with and always remember. So…

FOR THE BEST CHILDREN'S BOOKS,
LOOK FOR THE BEAR